Michael Arvaarluk Kusugak
HIDE AND SNEAK

Vladyana Krykorka

Annick Press

Annick Press Ltd.
Toronto, Canada

Annick Press gratefully acknowledges the support of The
Canada Council and the Ontario Arts Council

The Author thanks the Ontario Arts Council for helping him
find the time to finish this story.

Graphic design by Vladyana Krykorka

Canadian Cataloguing in Publication Data

Kusugak, Michael
  Hide and sneak, hide and sneak

ISBN 1-55037-229-7 (bound)   ISBN 1-55037-228-9 (pbk.)

1. Inuit—Juvenile fiction.*   I. Krykorka, Vladyana.
II. Title.

PS8571.U78H5 1992   jC813'.54   C91-095479-8
PZ7.K87Hi 1992

Distribution for Canada and the USA:
Firefly Books Ltd.
250 Sparks Avenue
North York, Ontario
M2H 2S4   Canada

Printed and bound in Canada
by D.W. Friesen & Sons

∞ Printed on acid free stock

To my wife, Sandra, with love   M.K.

For my friends in Rankin Inlet   V.K.

THE IJIRAQ AND THE INUKSUGAQ

There was once an Ijiraq who, like all other Ijiraqs, loved to play hide-and-seek. But, most of all, he liked to help little kids hide and, when he hid little kids, they were never ever found again. That is, of course, what Ijiraqs do: they help you hide, and when they help you hide, no one ever finds you again.

But our Ijiraq was a little different from other Ijiraqs; he was always getting lost. Whenever he went out to hide kids, he could not find his way home. And his friends teased him:

> Funny little Ijiraq
> Getting lost among the rocks
> Naa-na-na-na-naa . . .

He was so embarrassed. One day he decided to build an inuksugaq (which is sometimes called an ''inukshuk'') near his home. On a hill, he piled big heavy rocks on top of each other until it looked like a man, standing. Inuksugaqs were built in a long line to corral caribou to a place where they could be hunted, but our Ijiraq used his to help him find his way home. And he never got lost again.

And, to this very day, that is what inuksugaqs are used for, to help you find your way home. But that is another story . . .

ᐅᑉᐱᕆᑕᐅᔪᖅ

One fine summer day, Allashua said, "I am going out to play hide-and-seek, Mom."

Her mother said, "Don't go too far away. An Ijiraq might hide you, and if an Ijiraq hides you, no one will ever find you again."

ᐅᑭᐅᖅ ᑕᐅᑉᐳᖅ

"Yes Mom," Allashua said and went out of her tent into the sunshine. Tiny flowers covered the ground and the water on the lake behind her tent was so still she could see the sky in it. A loon made a long "V" in the water as it swam on the lake. On the sea in front of her tent, the floats on a net were lined up neatly in the still water. When all the floats are floating on the water there are no fish in the nets. They were all floating.

On a hill, an inuksugaq stood quietly looking out over the land and sea. It had to stand quietly because it was made of rocks, piled one on top of the other to look like a man. Allashua looked at it and wondered why anyone would pile big, heavy rocks on top of each other to look like a man. She said to herself, "I'll have to remember to ask my father what it is for." But, of course, she forgot.

She ran off to play hide-and-seek with her friends.

Allashua loved to play hide-and-seek but she was not very good at it. As she skipped along looking for a place to hide, a bright yellow butterfly fluttered by and Allashua ran after it, yelling, ''Qitusuk, qitusuk, qitusuk . . .'' That is, of course, the way you make a butterfly so tired it will fall down so you can catch it. But, soon, Allashua got so tired she had to stop and sit down. And she forgot to hide. Allashua was not very good at hide-and-seek.

W hen Allashua was looking for a place to hide again she came to a pond beside a rocky hill. Tiny prickly fish darted across the pond floor and disappeared under the rocks. She stopped to take a closer look. There was a big black bug crawling along the pond floor. It looked like a beetle just meandering along on its short black legs. Then there were tweeny, tiny fish that she thought looked like they did not have any skins at all. She could see their skeletons and all their insides. They swam around, just the same, without a care in the world. There were little, round, red bugs that moved about from here to there with no sign of any legs or fins. But she was most fascinated by the ulikapaalik, a tiny, turtle-like creature in a fragile-looking shell. It had a pointy tail and swam along by tickling the water with the many fingers on its undersides. Allashua watched these bugs for a long time. And she completely forgot to hide again.

And, again, she lost her turn. She was not very good at hide-and-seek.

Later, when Allashua was looking for a place to hide, she came upon a nest of tiny baby birds. The baby birds lifted their tiny beaks up to her and chirped, "Cheep, cheep, cheep, cheep . . ."

Allashua got on her knees, puckered up her lips and replied, "Cheep, cheep, cheep . . ."

And, from somewhere behind her, Allashua heard some whistling and a tiny voice singing:

> *Hide-and-sneak, hide-and-sneak*
> *How I love to hide-and-sneak . . .*

ᐱᕐᖁᓯᕐᐱᐅᓯᖅ

ᐊᑦᑲᓇᑎᑕ

llashua looked around but there was no one there. There were rocks and flowers and Old-Squaw ducks on a lake, but they weren't whistling or singing. She scratched her head and went back to the little birds. She puckered-up her lips again to talk to them but, behind her, there was the little voice again:

> *Hide-and-sneak, hide-and-sneak*
> *How I love to hide-and-sneak*
> *I hide and you seek*
> *You won't find me for a week.*

Allashua looked around. She didn't see anybody but she heard the whistling and singing and laughing like someone was having a good time. She looked and looked and, finally, behind a big rock, she found a tiny little man. He was dressed in a fur coat that looked like ptarmigan feathers in summer. His brown legs were bare and he had nothing on his feet at all. Like a ptarmigan in summer, he was very hard to see. Allashua knew she had met an Ijiraq, a hide-and-seek creature.

The little man laughed and cackled and danced as he sang his little song. As soon as he saw Allashua, he skipped away to hide behind a rock but, as he did so, he tripped on the rock and went tumbling along the ground. Allashua laughed and ran after him. He was a shy little man, but soon he began to play with Allashua. He loved to play hide-and-seek and he was very good at it. Allashua said, "I am not very good at hiding."

The Ijiraq said, "I am very good at hiding. Let me help you."

Allashua thought, "This guy is an Ijiraq, and my mother said if an Ijiraq hides you, no one will ever find you again. But he is such a happy, fun-loving little man. Elves don't hide you forever; dwarves don't hide you forever; leprechauns don't hide you forever. I think my mother is wrong."

She said, "Okay."

Allashua and the Ijiraq skipped up the hill with the inuksugaq on it. As they skipped down the other side, the Ijiraq tripped on a rock again and went tumbling down. Allashua laughed and laughed. He was so funny. They skipped and sang across a rocky field. They skipped around a lake. They skipped and danced through a big field of cotton grass. Finally, they came to a small creek with fish fins sticking up out of the water. As they stepped into the water to skip across, the fish jumped and water splashed everywhere. They skipped across and hid in a cave that Allashua had never seen before. Allashua looked all around. She did not have the foggiest idea where they were. She asked, "Where are we? I have never seen this place before."

The Ijiraq replied, "We are in my special hiding place. Here no one will ever find us."

They hid. They hid for a long time. The Ijiraq beamed with pride at being such a good hider. Lunchtime came and went and still no one found them. The Ijiraq laughed and cackled and sang his little song. He was having a wonderful time. But Allashua was getting hungry. She decided no one would ever find them again and it suited the Ijiraq just fine. She said, "I want to go home now."

The Ijiraq replied, "But they haven't found us yet."

"I am hungry and I want to go home now!" Allashua insisted.

"Well, you can't!" the Ijiraq said, getting annoyed at Allashua.

ᐊᐅᔭᒃᓴᒥ

Allashua wanted to go home. She was getting awfully hungry and, now, she missed her mother too. But the Ijiraq was not going to let her go home. Then she had a terrific idea. She looked straight at the Ijiraq and said to him, "You look funny."

The Ijiraq looked at her and said, "Don't look at me!"

But Allashua kept right on staring at him. "Your nose is crooked," she said, teasing the Ijiraq.

The Ijiraq's face turned red; he was so shy. But Allashua kept staring straight at him. She could not look away now; if she did, she knew he would disappear. "Don't look at me!" he said again.

ou're a clumsy little oaf, always tripping over things," she said.

"Don't stare at me!" he said. His face was red hot.

"Only if you take me home," she said.

"No!" he said again.

"Red face, red face, reddest in the human race. Naa, na, na, na, na . . ." Allashua teased.

Well, the Ijiraq was so shy he could not stand it any longer. He said, "Okay, I'll take you home but don't stare at me anymore."

ᐊᐅᐸᖅᓯᓐ ᐖᕿᐳᐊᖅ ᖅ...

They left the cave. They skipped along again until they came to the tiny creek. There were the fish again, their fins sticking up out of the shallow water. Even before her feet touched the water, Allashua knew something was going to happen. But it was too late. She did not dare take her eyes away from the Ijiraq. They jumped into the water. The fish jumped up, splashing water everywhere. The water splashed on Allashua's dress, it splashed on Allashua's hair and it splashed into Allashua's eyes. Allashua blinked. When she opened her eyes, the Ijiraq was gone. Poof. Gone. Just like that.

Allashua looked around but the Ijiraq was nowhere to be found. She looked everywhere. Still there was no Ijiraq. Allashua was alone. And she didn't know where she was. She was lost.

Allashua began to cry, "Waah, I want my Mommy . . . Waa-ah, I want to go home . . ."

She cried for a long time but no one came. She cried until her eyes turned as red as the Ijiraq's face. She cried until she had no cry left in her body. Then, finally, she stopped crying.

Allashua didn't know what to do. She looked all around. Way, way far away, so far away she could hardly see it, there was a black dot on a hill. It was the only thing she saw on the horizon. Allashua wondered what it was. She said to herself, "I am going to go there."

She started to walk. She walked across a field of cotton grass. The black dot on the hill looked a little bigger. She skipped around a lake. Now the black dot on the hill seemed to be standing. She skipped and danced across a large rocky field. Now the dot looked like a man standing on the hill. She went up the hill and walked over to it. It was an inuksugaq, standing quietly, looking out over the land and sea. She said, "I have seen this inuksugaq before." She looked around to where the inuksugaq was looking. There was a river, there was the sea and the land and, way down on the shore, there was a tent. She looked and looked at the tent. It was her tent. She was so happy. She said, "Thank you," to the inuksugaq and skipped and ran all the way home.

ᗡᑊ ᑕᗅᑕᗡᕿᑊᒍᐸᔆᒋ

Her mother and father and brothers and sisters were so happy to see her. They hugged her and kissed her and asked, "Where have you been, Allashua? We have been worried about you."

"On the other side of the hill playing hide-and-seek," she replied.

She told them about playing hide-and-seek, she told them about the Ijiraq and she told them about being lost. Then she asked her father, "Father, what is an inuksugaq for?"

"To help you find your way home," he replied.

She said, "You know what, Father? It works."

When Allashua saw her friends again they said she was such a good hider. They had looked for her everywhere but they could not find her. Allashua was pretty proud. She still loved to play hide-and-seek and she still was not very good at it, but she really didn't mind. There were always butterflies to chase and tiny bugs to look at. It was fun anyway. And she always sang a little song:

Hide-and-sneak, hide-and-sneak
How I love to hide-and-sneak
I hide and you seek
You won't find me for a week.

And she never, ever, saw an Ijiraq again. Ijiraqs are so hard to see, just like ptarmigan in summer.

Taima